*The Glo Friends live in a magical place called
Glo Land. This colourful rhyming story tells of one
of their adventures.*

British Library Cataloguing in Publication Data

Woodman, June
    Glo Bug.—(Glo friends; 4)
    I. Title   II. Thompson, Carole
    III. Series
    823'.914[J]   PZ7
    ISBN 0-7214-0980-6

First edition

Published by Ladybird Books Ltd Loughborough Leicestershire UK
Ladybird Books Inc Lewiston Maine 04240 USA

GLO Friends™

GLO Bug's greatest day

written by JUNE WOODMAN
illustrated by CAROLE THOMPSON

Ladybird Books

Glo Bug is a jolly friend,
As happy as can be.
His greatest friend is Glo Worm in
The Glo Land family.

He thinks Glo Worm is brilliant,
And brave and daring too.
Yet sometimes Glo Bug thinks he'd like
To show what *he* can do.

When Moondrops fall, he's never first
To find where they descend.
But If a Glo Friend needs a hand,
On Glo Bug they depend.

He always holds the ladder firm
While Glo Worm paints for hours.
He does the boring digging, but
Glo Spider picks the flowers.

He gets stuck with the washing-up
For Glo Grannybug's huge meals.
They all take him for granted, he's
Quite put-upon, he feels.

"I'll show them all," he mutters, but
The question is, just how?
Glo Grannybug is calling him,
But Glo Bug says, "Not now!"

Glo Grannybug is *most* surprised
To get such a reply.
Then Glo Worm says, "He seems so sad,"
And they both wonder why.

As Glo Bug heads off for the woods,
Glo Butterfly calls out,
"Please will you come and cut my lawn?"
"***Not now***!" she hears him shout.

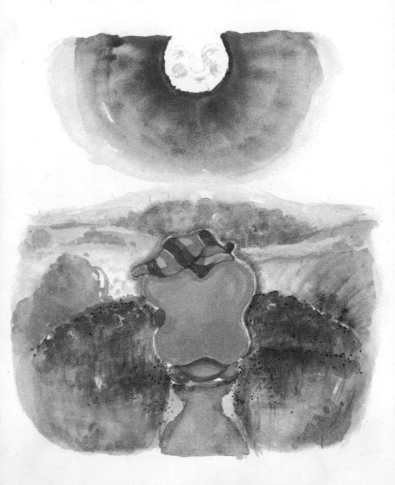

Glo Snail looks up as he goes past
And says, "My garden needs
A good hard-working bug like you.
Please pull up all my weeds."

But Glo Bug crossly shakes his head,
"**No**. Not today," says he.
"There's something I must think about
So kindly let me be!"

Glo Snail is quite astonished
To be spoken to that way.
He goes to ask Glo Grannybug,
"What's wrong with *him* today?"

Now he's alone, poor Glo Bug finds
A peaceful little place
Deep in the woods, where he sits down
With such a long, sad face.

It's quiet in the leafy woods,
Except for buzzing bees
And sleepy twitters from the birds,
As they rest in the trees.

Sad Glo Bug's head begins to nod,
He curls up with a sigh.
And soon he starts to dream that he
Is flying in the sky.

But he is not alone up there,
Some witches fly right past,
Riding on their broomsticks
And going very fast.

The witches are both yelling,
And one is heard to say,
"Do hurry, or we'll be too late
To raid Glo Land today!"

Poor Glo Bug wonders what to do
To stop this fearsome raid.
He flies as fast as he can fly
To go to Glo Land's aid.

But even as he rushes on
He knows it is too late.
Arriving in a temper he
Finds things in *such* a state.

Glo Grannybug's good food is all
Tipped out upon the ground.
Glo Pond is full of rubbish, and
Glo Worm is gagged and bound.

But just as Glo Bug rushes in
To set poor Glo Worm free,
He's suddenly surprised to find
He's on a ship, at sea!

At first, he's feeling happy as
He sails out in the sun.
But then he spies a *pirate* ship –
It's carrying a gun!

That pirate ship is heading straight
For Glo Bug, and he thinks,
"If there's a fight, I know *my* ship
Will be the one that sinks!"

Poor Glo Bug's knees are knocking as
The pirates yell and scream...
Then suddenly he's in the midst
Of quite a different dream!

This time he's out in cowboy land
Beside a sun-baked rock.
But then fierce bandits make a raid –
Oh, what a nasty shock!

He does his best to run, but there's
A hand upon his arm.
What will those bandits do to him?
He's done them all no harm.

Now all at once he wakes – to find
Himself beneath the tree.
Young Glo Worm's holding on to him
As he tries to break free.

Now Glow Worm smiles, "Those *were* bad
  dreams,"
And helps him to his feet.
"Come on, my friend, for we all think
That you deserve a treat."

"No treat will cheer *me*," Glo Bug thinks,
"I'm just no good it seems.
I'll never be a hero brave,
Not even in my dreams."

Still feeling dreary he plods off
As Glo Worm leads the way.
Back home, Glo Grannybug says, "Be
Our king – just for one day!"

So early the next morning when
Glo Bug rolls out of bed,
His subjects are all waiting as
Glo Grannybug had said!

Glo Spider's made a cloak for him
Of very finest silk.
Glo Grannybug then serves him with
Some cornflakes, egg and milk.

They hold a Coronation,
Beside the Glo Pond blue.
Glo Butterfly now crowns Glo Bug
And asks what they must do.

Oh, what a lovely feeling for
Glo Bug has been so sad.
This day is just the greatest one
That he has ever had.

He sends the Glo Friends scurrying
To carry out each wish –
To paint, or mow, or weed, or cook
A really royal dish.

The Glo Friends all work very hard
To do the 'king's' commands.
They all end up with aching backs,
And feet, *and* knees, *and hands*!

As daylight softly fades away
The Glo Friends shine so bright.
Then smiling Glo Bug says, "I won't
Have nasty dreams tonight!"

So ever after that, if he
Starts feeling rather sad,
He smiles, and just remembers the
Best day he ever had!